BASKETBALL WAR

by Jonny Zucker

illustrated by
Paul Savage

Librarian Reviewer
Joanne Bongaarts
Educational Consultant
MS in Library Media Education, Minnesota State University, Mankato, MN
Teacher and Media Specialist with Edina Public Schools, MN, 1993–2000

Reading Consultant
Elizabeth Stedem
Educator/Consultant, Colorado Springs, CO
MA in Elementary Education, University of Denver, CO

STONE ARCH BOOKS
Minneapolis   San Diego

First published in the United States in 2006
by Stone Arch Books,
151 Good Counsel Drive, P.O. Box 669,
Mankato, Minnesota 56002.
www.stonearchbooks.com

Originally published in Great Britain in 2004
by Badger Publishing Ltd.

Original work copyright © 2004 Badger Publishing Ltd
Text copyright © 2004 Jonny Zucker

Library of Congress Cataloging-in-Publication Data
Zucker, Jonny.
    Basketball War / by Jonny Zucker; illustrated by Paul Savage.
    p. cm. — Keystone Books.
    Summary: When their arch-rivals get a new coach mid-season—
and
an entirely new team—basketball team captain Jim and his best friend
Ali do some investigating that uncovers a sinister plot.
    ISBN-13: 978-1-59889-009-9 (hardcover)
    ISBN-10: 1-59889-009-3 (hardcover)
    ISBN-13: 978-1-59889-181-2 (paperback)
    ISBN-10: 1-59889-181-2 (paperback)
    [1. Basketball—Fiction. 2. Contests—Fiction. 3. Extraterrestrial
beings—Fiction.] I. Savage, Paul, 1971– ill. II. Title.
PZ7.Z77925Bas 2006
[Fic]—dc22
2005026335

1 2 3 4 5 6 11 10 09 08 07 06

Printed in the United States of America

TABLE OF CONTENTS

Chapter 1

CHECK OUT

All season, the Western Lions were the league's top team. Their captain, Jim Davis, and his best friend, Ali, were the team's best players.

The Lions' closest rivals, the Langham Jets, lost their first five games. Before their sixth game, the Jets hired a new coach, Mr. Hunt. Coach Hunt got rid of all of the old players and selected a brand new team.

Some of the former Jets players went to school with Jim and Ali. They said they were furious that Coach Hunt kicked them off the team. They also said that they didn't know any of the new players Coach Hunt added to the team.

As soon as Coach Hunt arrived, the Jets started winning and catching up to the Lions. With one game left, the Lions and the Jets were tied. In just over two weeks, they would face each other in the championship game.

* * *

"Let's go check out the Jets after school," Jim said to Ali. "We'll see how good they are."

The boys rode a bus to Langham Park and then headed to the sports center. They walked toward the outdoor basketball court, talking about the Jets.

Suddenly, a man blocked their way. He was very tall with a harsh face, and he was carrying a large metal case.

"Why are you talking about the Jets?" he asked angrily.

Jim and Ali stared at him, surprised.

"Who are you?" asked Ali.

"I'm Coach Hunt," the man replied, "and I don't like people spying on my team."

"We're not spying," said Jim.

"Yeah," added Ali, "and, anyway, it's a free country."

"Not around here, it's not," snapped Coach Hunt. "Now get out of here before you regret it!"

Jim was going to reply, but Ali tugged at his arm.

The boys turned and walked away. As they got close to the gate, Jim turned around. Coach Hunt was standing in exactly the same place, holding the metal case tightly, and staring at him with hate-filled eyes.

Chapter 2

DARKNESS

The next Wednesday, Jim and Ali returned to Langham Park. They were not going to be scared off by Coach Hunt. They hid in some bushes behind the basketball court.

Coach Hunt was running a practice drill. His metal case was on the ground next to him. The Jets looked good. They passed and shot with great skill and speed.

When one of the players seemed
tired, Coach Hunt took something out
of the metal case and handed it to
him. The boy put it in his mouth, and
he was suddenly full of energy again.

"Must be one of those energy bars,"
Ali whispered.

Jim and Ali watched the practice
for over an hour. It was getting too
dark to see, but they could still hear
the practice going on.

"How can they play?" asked Ali. "It's almost pitch black."

"I don't know," replied Jim. "Something weird is going on."

Ali checked his watch.

"I can't stay any longer," he said. "I need to get home."

"Me, too," nodded Jim, "but we need to find out more about Coach Hunt and his team."

They crept out of the bushes and headed toward the bus stop. As they hurried out of the park, they could hear Coach Hunt shouting at his players in the dark.

Chapter 3

THE TURN DOWN

On Saturday afternoon, Jim and Ali walked to the mall.

"What are we going to do about the Jets?" Ali asked as they looked at some basketball shoes.

"I've got an idea," Jim replied. "The referee for the championship game is Fred Samson. My uncle knows him from school. They used to play basketball together."

"He lives around the corner," Jim added. "Why don't we go and tell him that something's up with the Jets?"

Ali smiled. "Nice one," he said. "Let's go there now."

They quickly found the house and rang the bell.

After a few seconds, the door opened, and Fred Samson stood there in a running suit, staring at them.

"Yes?" he asked.

"Hi," said Jim. "We both play for the Western Lions, and we'd like to talk to you about the Jets and their coach."

Fred Samson stopped Jim by holding up his hand.

"Look, you two," he said quietly. "I'm the referee for the game."

"We know," said Jim. "That's why we're here. We've been watching Coach Hunt and his team. We think there's something strange going on."

Fred shook his head.

"You shouldn't have come here!" he snapped. "If anyone sees you, they'll think you're trying to cheat. I can't talk to you about the game."

"But —" started Ali.

"No buts," hissed Mr. Samson. "Just go away!"

Jim and Ali slowly turned away as the door slammed shut behind them.

Chapter 4

THE FOLLOW UP

It was Wednesday night. The game against the Jets was on Saturday.

Jim and Ali waited outside the gates of Langham Park. They could hear Coach Hunt shouting in the distance. The Jets were finishing up their practice.

Five minutes later, one of the Jets walked through the gates and right past them.

"Let's follow him," whispered Jim.

The Jets player headed up to the main street and crossed it. Jim and Ali were close behind.

"Why are we following him?" Ali asked.

"He might lead us to a clue about the Jets," Jim replied.

The Jets player took a left and began to walk along a dark path by an old factory.

"Where's he going?" asked Ali.

"Don't know," replied Jim.

The Jets player suddenly turned down a narrow alley. Jim and Ali ran to keep up with him. As soon as they reached the entrance to the alley, they both stopped in shock.

The Jets player was nowhere to be seen. He had vanished.

Chapter 5

AN EARLY MOVER

Saturday finally arrived, the day of the championship game.

Jim and Ali spent hours talking about Coach Hunt, the practices in the dark, and the vanishing Jets player. They still didn't have any answers.

That morning, Jim was looking out of his bedroom window when he saw Coach Hunt walk past.

The Jets coach was hurrying in the direction of Western Park. He was carrying his metal case.

Jim checked his watch. It was only noon — three hours before the game's start. He ran outside, grabbed his bike, and pedaled as fast as he could to Ali's house.

"What's up?" asked Ali as he opened his front door.

"I've just seen Coach Hunt heading toward the park!" shouted Jim. "We've got to do something."

Ali grabbed his bike, and they sped along to Fred Samson's house.

Jim rang the bell three times.

Finally, the door opened a crack, and Fred Samson looked out.

"I told you boys to stay away!" he said angrily.

"This is really important, Mr. Samson," Jim said.

Fred Samson looked down at them with fury.

"I've already told you once!" he shouted. "Stay away from me! I'll see you both later at the game."

"Maybe we're going too far," Ali said to Jim as they turned away from Fred Samson's house.

"No way," replied Jim. "This is only the beginning."

Chapter 6

THE LOCKER ROOM

Jim and Ali reached the sports
center at Western Park and climbed off
their bikes.

The windows were too high for them
to see anything, but they could hear
Coach Hunt's voice coming from one
of the locker rooms inside.

"We've learned about basketball,"
he was saying. "Next, we'll need to
find out about a thing called baseball."

"When we know everything about these sports," Coach Hunt continued, "we'll be able to take over this planet."

"Quick! Over here," whispered Jim. He was making a pile of bricks to stand on. He and Ali climbed up and looked through the window.

Neither could believe what they saw.

Inside the locker room were one large and eleven medium-sized, light-blue, slimy creatures. The large creature reached inside the metal case and pulled out a disk. He put it into his mouth. As soon as he'd done this, he immediately looked like Coach Hunt. He took out more disks and passed them around.

As each blue creature placed a disk in its mouth, it took on human form. They were the Jets players!

Coach Hunt spoke again. "Remember that these disks can make you look human for only six hours."

"If any of you are seen without your human cover, then we have failed and will have to return home," Coach Hunt continued. "Our research will stop, and the war will be delayed. Does everyone understand?"

All of the Jets players nodded, but at that moment, a loud thud sounded outside the locker room.

The Jets players and Coach Hunt all looked up to see the faces of Jim and Ali hitting the locker room window as their tower of bricks fell over.

There was a sudden bang, and then the locker room was filled with smoke.

Chapter 7

A SPEEDY EXIT

"Quick!" yelled Jim.

They jumped down and rushed into the locker room.

The smoke was so thick that it was about 30 seconds before they could see anything.

"I don't believe it!" shouted Jim as the smoke began to clear.

The locker room was completely empty except for the large metal case resting on the floor. As Jim picked it up, they suddenly heard a loud humming noise coming from outside.

They ran out and stared up at the sky. Flying at great speed, a giant black craft headed swiftly toward the clouds and then disappeared.

Chapter 8

VICTORY

Jim and Ali sat on a bench, talking over what they'd just seen.

"It all makes sense," said Ali. "The players being able to see in the dark, the disks, and the boy who vanished in that alley."

"It still doesn't seem real," replied Jim. "It's like something out of a science fiction movie."

"What's that about a movie?"

Jim and Ali looked up. It was Fred Samson in his referee uniform.

"We've been trying to tell you for two weeks," said Jim, staring at Fred.

"Well, I'm here now," said Fred. "So tell me what this is all about."

The boys told him everything, from their first meeting with Coach Hunt to the craft flying off into space.

"Do you believe us?" Ali asked when they'd finished talking.

"Have you got any proof?" Fred wanted to know.

Jim nodded and pulled out the metal case from under the bench.

Fred reached out and took the case. He looked at it for a few moments and turned it around several times.

"I do believe you," Fred said, "and I'll tell you what I'm going to do. I'll take this case to the police and explain what happened. They're far more likely to listen to me than the two of you."

"Well, can we at least come with you?" asked Jim.

At that moment, the rest of the Lions players started arriving.

"Go celebrate," smiled Fred. "Your team just won the championship!"

Jim got all of the Lions players together and told them that the Jets were a no-show. The game wouldn't happen. The Lions had won the championship. The Lions players were puzzled at first, but they soon started cheering. They were the league champions!

After a few minutes, Jim called Ali over. "Have you seen Fred?" he asked.

Ali shook his head. "He must have left for the police station."

"Yeah," nodded Jim, "you're probably right."

Jim and Ali followed the rest of the Lions out of the park.

* * *

At the other end of the park, Fred Samson was walking away, gripping the metal case. He moved to the shelter of some trees and put the case down.

His face was starting to turn a light-blue color. He quickly opened the case, pulled out a disk, and placed it carefully into his mouth.

ABOUT THE AUTHOR

Even as a child, Jonny Zucker wanted to be a writer. Today, he has written more than 30 books. He has also spent time working as a teacher, song writer, and stand-up comedian. Jonny lives in London with his wife and two children.

ABOUT THE ILLUSTRATOR

Paul Savage works in a design studio, drawing pictures for advertising. He says illustrating books is "the best job." He's always been interested in illustrating books, and he loves reading. Paul also enjoys playing sports and running.

He lives in England with his wife and daughter, Amelia.

GLOSSARY

craft (KRAFT)—a vehicle, such as a boat, spaceship, or plane

fury (FYUR-ee)—violent anger or rage

league (LEEG)—a group of people with a common interest or activity, such as a group of basketball teams that play against each other

referee (ref-uh-REE)—someone who supervises a sports match or a game, and makes sure that players obey the rules

rival (RYE-vuhl)—someone you compete against

DISCUSSION QUESTIONS

1. When Jim and Ali follow the Jets player after practice, the player seems to just disappear. Where do you think he went?

2. If Jim and Ali told their teammates about the aliens, do you think the team would believe them? Why or why not?

3. At the end of the story, we find out that Fred Samson is an alien. What do you think he's going to do next?

WRITING PROMPTS

1. Do you believe in aliens? Do you think aliens might someday visit Earth? Write about what aliens might look like and what they would do if they came to Earth.

2. If you thought someone was behaving strangely, would you investigate like Jim and Ali did? Write a story about how you would investigate someone, and what you discovered about them.

3. If you could change your form by putting a disk in your mouth, would you? Describe what you would change into and why?

ALSO BY
JONNY ZUCKER

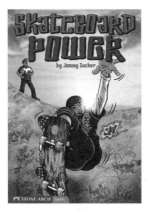

Skateboard Power

The skateboarding competition is just two weeks away, and Nick knows he's got a great shot at winning. But then the meanest kid in school tells Nick to stay out of the competition or else.

Steel Eyes

Emma Stone is the new girl in school. Why does she always wear sunglasses? Gail and Tanya are determined to find out, but Emma's cold stare is more than they bargained for.